WAR GAMES

WAR GAMES

James Riordan
Illustrated by Jane Cope

A & C BLACK
AN IMPRINT OF BLOOMSBURY
LONDON NEW DELHI NEW YORK SYDNEY

White Wolves Series Consultant: Sue Ellis,
Centre for Literacy in Primary Education

This book can be used in the White Wolves Guided Reading programme
with children who have an average level of reading experience at Year 4 level

First published 2008 by
A & C Black Publishers Ltd,
an imprint of Bloomsbury Publishing Plc
50 Bedford Square, London, WC1B 3DP

www.bloomsbury.com

ISBN 978-0-7136-8750-7

10 9 8 7 6 5

A CIP catalogue for this book is available from the British Library.

MIX
Paper from
responsible sources
FSC® C013604

Printed and bound in Great Britain
by CPI Group (UK) Ltd, Croydon, CR0 4YY

CONTENTS

CONTENTS

CHAPTER ONE

It was the clearest, most beautiful night of the year, as still and pure as Christmas should be. Christmas Eve, 1914. The first Christmas that 18-year-old Jack and Harry had spent away from home.

There was a war on. Some called it the Great War because it was the first time the whole world had gone to war. British soldiers had been sent to France to stop the Germans crossing the sea to England.

It was snowing. A thin, white sheet covered the naked earth of No Man's Land. No Man's Land was a good name: no man dared cross it. Those who'd tried lay stiff and torn like twisted thorn trees. The earth was full of frosty water holes, used shells and barbed wire glinting in the winter sun.

At either end, half a football
pitch apart, were trenches; deep
enough for men to stand in
without having their heads blown
off; long enough to drag away
the dead and wounded. Soldiers
peered over the top, rifles at the
ready, on the look-out for the
enemy.

In one trench were the British in stiff, round hats, jackets, and trousers as brown as mud. In the other were Germans in uniforms of olive green. Both sides stood ankle-deep in water. Now and then, big, black rats sniffed their boots in search of food.

All at once, in the dark of evening, a strange sound drifted across No Man's Land. It was coming from the German trenches – a sort of humming noise like a swarm of honeybees.

Harry turned to Jack. "Listen. It sounds like a singsong."

The singing rose and dipped like a swallow in summer skies.

"'Silent Night', isn't it?" said Jack.

He smiled in recognition. It reminded him of Sunday school when he was little. At Christmas, girls and boys would sing carols for the grown-ups.

It made him sad to think of home: Mum, Dad and the twins, Maisie and Daisie.

"Let's give them a carol back," suggested Harry. "How about 'Once in Royal David's City'?"

Jack and Harry raised their voices, *dum-dum-dumming* to the words they forgot. Other soldiers took up the tune. When they ran out of words, there was a pause, before clapping came from the trenches opposite.

A German voice shouted, "Bravo, Tommy!"

Back bounced the Germans. A single bass voice sang out before a choir of male voices joined in with 'O, Come All Ye Faithful'.

The British heard it through, then gave a cheer.

"Very nice, Jerry!"

"Come on, boys, we can do better than that," shouted Sergeant Morris down the line. "Let's teach them to sing 'Silent Night' properly."

The sergeant had grown up in the coalfields of South Wales, singing in a chapel choir. His deep voice cut through the still, silent night. Then English and German voices took up the song. And the two choirs, friend and foe, sang together. First sweet and low, then climbing up to the starry skies.

In the hush that followed, no man dared break the magic spell. For a few minutes, there was deathly silence.

Then, all at once, a German voice rang out:

"Hey, Tommy, Merry Christmas!"

On both sides, voices took up the cry.

"Happy Christmas!"

"*Fröhliche Weihnachten!*"

Then loud cheering and clapping. The grim space of No Man's Land was full of friendship and goodwill – to all men, Tommy and Jerry alike.

CHAPTER TWO

In the darkness, a German voice
cut through the frosty air.

"Hey, Englisher! What about
a bit of peace at Christmas?
No more shooting, *ja*?"

For a while, the British trenches fell silent. Since the officers had gone to Christmas dinner behind the lines, there was no one in charge. What were they to do? The Germans were the enemy, after all.

Then the loud voice of Sergeant Morris rang out: "Right, I'll take over. OK, boys?"

The roar that met his shout expressed the feelings of men at war. Soldiers had made themselves heard above the guns on both sides of the front.

To the Germans, Sergeant Morris shouted out, "Fine with us. No firing at Christmas. You have my word."

At that, more songs were sung. A German played a tune on his mouth organ before voices took up the chorus: *O, Tannenbaum.*

As the song died away, a Scottish soldier in a tartan kilt stood on the bank and played the bagpipes. Goodness knows what the Germans made of that. But the Scot got the biggest cheer of the night, from both sets of trenches.

Jack's thoughts turned again
to home. He wondered if Maisie
had received his last letter. The one
where he reminded her to feed his
rabbits. "They like dandelion and
dock leaves best," he'd said. "Don't
forget to give them clean straw
once a week."

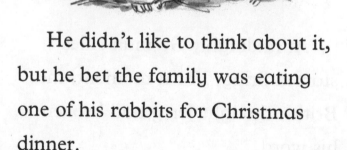

He didn't like to think about it,
but he bet the family was eating
one of his rabbits for Christmas
dinner.

He could see them all clearly
in his mind's eye, sitting round the
table, Dad saying, "Here's to our
Jack. May he come home soon."

At midnight, German rifles
started firing. For a moment, the
British thought Jerry had broken
his word.

But, no: the shots were to greet Christmas Day. The British fired into the air, too.

A hundred yards apart, men waved torches and wished each other 'Merry Christmas'.

"To you, too, Mum and Dad,"
said Jack under his breath.

He knew that they would be
pleased if they could see how
Christmas had brought friend
and foe together as one big family
that night.

CHAPTER THREE

Christmas Day dawned crisp
and clear.

Jack was dreaming of home,
his family sitting round the fire,
unwrapping presents and pulling
crackers. He sat up with a jolt.
Had a cracker woken him?

No, it was Sergeant Morris.

"Action stations! Take aim.
Fire when I give the word!"

A hundred men trained their rifles on a lone figure in green uniform and postman's hat.

He was walking slowly across the ground, dragging something behind him. What was it? A bomb? A gun? A secret weapon?

"Well, bless me," cried the sergeant. "He's planting a Christmas tree, right in the middle of No Man's Land!"

The German soldier had made a hole with his bare hands and was planting a fir tree. Its topmost branches brushed his chest. Then, standing to attention, he saluted the tree, turned smartly about and marched back the way he'd come.

"He's a brave lad," said Sergeant Morris. "I could have blown him to bits."

"Daft as a brush," said Harry. "You wouldn't catch one of our lads acting so silly."

Just then a figure in brown stood up.

"Get down, you idiot," hissed Sergeant Morris, "before they blow your head off!"

But the man stood calm and still.

"What's that in his hands, a Christmas pudding?" said Harry.

The men stared in alarm as

the soldier took a run and kicked the 'pudding' high into the air. It bounced twice, high and fast on the crusty soil, before plopping – *Splosh*! – right into an icy puddle.

"How about a game of football?" the kicker yelled.

"Right, you're on, pal," cried Jack. "Come on, lads. We started the game. Let's show those Germans how to play it."

Harry, Jack and a dozen others followed Archie, the ball's owner, out into No Man's Land.

At first the Germans stood and stared.

"*Dummköpfe*! Crazy English!"

Before they'd even kicked off, a bunch of Germans in shirtsleeves came rushing over the top.

One red-faced fellow with ginger hair was shouting, "Hey, Tommy, what about a game? You and us, *ja*? Germany versus England."

Archie turned to his mates.

"What about it, lads?"

Nods and grins greeted the cry.

"You're on, Jerry," Archie shouted back.

Cheers and shouts on both sides welcomed the match.

One soldier yelled above the noise, "Why don't we play to end the war? Then we can all go home."

"Yes," added another, "and have a game each year to decide European champions. It'll save a lot of lives."

Sergeant Morris's foghorn voice cut through the cries. "Clear the pitch first. Bury the dead."

It was only right and proper.

The Germans carried their dead comrades off. The British did the same. It wasn't a pleasant task. But you can't play football with dead bodies everywhere.

Men then set to removing the barbed wire and empty shells from the strip of land. When, finally, a large enough space was cleared, they chose captains and picked sides.

Since it was Archie's ball, they let him be captain for England. Fair enough. No one minded. The ginger German captained their team.

Eleven a side. Green Shirts versus Brown Shirts. All wore trousers and boots, shirts and braces. Jackets and helmets marked the goals. There were no white lines, no referee, no whistle, no set time.

"First to five goals?" suggested Archie.

Green Shirts agreed. Before a ball was kicked, however, the two teams posed for a photo. It was to be a keepsake of the match:

ENGLAND V. GERMANY
25 DECEMBER 1914

CHAPTER FOUR

England kicked off. Red cheeks puffed out like rosy apples. Beads of sweat trickled down shiny necks. Steam curled up from backs in the crisp, morning air.

It was mostly kick and rush, with four or five bodies charging after the brown, leather ball. Despite the rough and tumble, there was never a fairer game. If someone was knocked over, his opponent stopped to help him up.

"Sorry, mate."

"Excuse me, comrade."

Above the grunts and cries of players rose two sets of chants from watching fans:

"ENG – LAND! ENG – LAND!"

"DEUTSCH – LAND! DEUTSCH – LAND!"

Players did as best they could in the mushy snow. The ball kept stopping dead as men rushed past, or the ball squirted into water holes. Men slipped and slid all over the place. Germany's captain had to pull Archie out of a shell hole, dripping wet.

Soon you couldn't tell friend from foe as green and brown turned to the colour of mud. All the fear and horror of war melted away in the Christmas fun.

As Harry said to Jack, "It's much better than killing each other, isn't it?"

When Germany went 4–2 up, the green ranks tossed their caps into the air and cheered as if they'd won the war.

Yet next time he was in front of the goal, the German captain did a strange thing. Instead of shooting, he picked up the ball and went over to Archie.

"It's Christmas," he said. "Who cares who wins? Let's mix up the teams and let everyone play. What do you say?"

Archie readily agreed. "Good idea. Winning isn't everything. Muddy Boots play Dirty Dogs."

Both captains waved their
arms towards the lines, calling up
reserves. The long and the short
and the tall, even those with arms
in slings and bandaged heads
joined in.

As brown-green men crowded
round the Christmas tree, the two
captains picked their teams. Two
from one side, then two from the

other – so that both sides
had roughly equal numbers
of British and Germans.

Forty-one Muddy Boots
against 42 Dirty Dogs.

Maybe that was the final
score – 41–42 – though no one kept
count. After an hour or so,
the ball landed smack-bang
on a German spiked helmet:
POOOFFF... All the air hissed out.

By that time the men had
had enough. Tired and happy,
steaming like boiling kettles, they
shook hands and beamed all over
their muddy faces.

As they were trooping off the
pitch, Archie gave a shout:

"Three cheers for Jerry. Hip-
Hip-Hooray! Hip-Hip-Hooray!
Hip-Hip-Hooray!"

The German captain followed
suit, and German cheers followed
the British from the pitch.

Soon soldiers were returning
to the field of play, exchanging
presents: cigarettes for chocolate,
sausage for bully beef, cake for
a woolly hat. Jack got chatting
to Fritz, the German captain,
who showed him a creased photo
from his pocket.

"My wife and children," he said.

Jack looked at a young woman with long, fair plaits, smiling nervously out of the brown photo. Two serious-looking children were tugging at her skirts on either side.

"That's nice," said Jack. "Here, I've a photo of Mum and Dad and my kid sisters. We're going to have a party once we've won the... Well, you know, when this lot's over."

He pulled a picture out of his pocket and turned it over. The words 'To Jack. Love, Sis xxx' were written at the bottom.

The German smiled. "What is your name?" he asked.

"Jack. Jack Hunt. And you?"

"Fritz. Fritz Krueger."

They gave each other a broad grin and shook hands warmly.

Just then a sudden flurry of snow brought the post-match party to an end.

"Thanks, Fritz. See you again some time."

"*Ja*. Happy Christmas, Jack."

Soldiers were hurrying back to the trenches, waving goodbye.

"Quite a nice bunch of lads," said Jack.

"Those English aren't so bad, after all," Fritz told his mate.

CHAPTER FIVE

When the officers returned from their Christmas dinner, they took a dim view of the football match. Soldiers had put their guns away. No sentry was on guard.

One said, "We've had enough of killing, we want to go home."

Something had to be done to restore order. Someone had to be punished.

Sergeant Morris had been in charge. So the officers stripped him of his three stripes and marched him off.

They arrested Archie too: he'd started the football match, after all. There was nothing Jack or Harry could do but stand by helplessly.

The men never saw Archie or Sergeant Morris again.

Somewhere, out of sight, they were tied to a post and shot.

On the other side of No Man's Land, the same thing happened.

"War must go on," said the British generals.

"War must go on," said the German generals.

At dawn on Boxing Day, 1914, the generals kept their word. As a cock crowed on a nearby farm, the war started up again.

The big guns boomed.

The bullets whizzed.

The shells showered down.

With dirt spurting all about, Jack dashed across the field, bayonet in hand. He'd seen Harry fall, an untidy row of red holes tearing his jacket front. Harry hadn't said a word, he'd just sunk slowly to the ground.

"Come on, matey," Jack had said, trying to help him up.

But there was nothing he could do. Harry was dead.

Jack stared, unbelieving. His best friend dead! What would he tell Harry's mum? Tears started in his eyes as he let go of the lifeless body.

He hurried on, firing blindly at the shadows ahead, jabbing at passing shapes, wishing he were home.

All at once, a flash exploded before his face and he stumbled – once, twice – falling senseless, down, down, down into a dark pit.

When he came to, the battle had passed. The field was oddly silent, as if players and fans had all gone home.

Then, all at once, he heard a voice. It was calling his name: "Jack, Jack..."

Through a red-stained mist, he looked about. Dimly, he made out another soldier in the shell hole.

"*Wasser*. Water."

It was Fritz, the German captain.

With his one good hand, Jack uncorked his water bottle and put it to Fritz's lips. The German's eyes closed as he gulped the water down, trying to put out the fire in his stomach.

"*Danke*. Thank you, Jack," he murmured through the pain.

They were his last words.

"That's OK, mate."

Jack took Fritz's cold hand in his as the German's eyes closed.

It seemed only hours since he'd shaken that same hand. Then it was warm; now it was cold.

Fritz was his team-mate. They'd all been friends together, kicking a football about. Yet now... Now Harry and Fritz were dead.

In football, they'd been the best of friends. In war, they were deadly foes.

This story is based on true events. Both British and German soldiers have talked of the 'Christmas truce' and the game of football that was part of it.

But the war went on for another four years, killing millions of men, far more than any war up till then. All the same, the events of Christmas 1914 – the carols and the football match – will go down as the most moving and inspiring of any war.

ABOUT THE AUTHOR

James Riordan is an award-winning children's writer and author of novels for young people – mostly on war.

For this book he visited the First World War museum in the Belgian town of Ypres, and read through hundreds of British and German letters sent home from the front. In addition, he consulted eyewitness accounts by soldiers about the 'Christmas truce'.

Other White Wolves Stories
With Historical Settings...

THE
QUEEN'S
TOKEN

Pamela Oldfield

Hal is a poor stable boy, who has
a dream – to work for King Henry
at his palace in Whitehall. But when
he chances upon the royal party, it's
not the meeting he'd hoped for. He's
accused of being a spy and his fate
now rests in the king's hands... Will
Henry live up to his fierce reputation,
or will Hal live another day?

The Queen's Token is a historical
story set in Tudor times.

ISBN: 9 780 7136 8850 4 £4.99

Other White Wolves Stories
With Historical Settings...

Outbreak

Alison Prince

Miriam doesn't understand why her
mum is buying more food than they
need, and storing it away. Or why her
parents have given her the nickname,
Mandy. Her friend Pam says it's
because war is coming. And, if the
Nazis invade, it will be dangerous
for her to have a Jewish name. But
that's not going to happen... Is it?

Outbreak is a historical story set
at the start of World War II.

ISBN: 9 780 7136 8840 5 £4.99

Year 4

Stories About Imagined Worlds

Stories That Raise Issues

Stories From Different Cultures

Historical Stories